MOTHER HOLLY

A RETELLING FROM THE

BROTHERS GRIMM BY

John Warren Stewig

WITH ILLUSTRATIONS BY

Johanna Westerman

A CHESHIRE STUDIO BOOK

North-South Books

NEW YORK 🍎 LONDON

In memory of Anneliese Kolb-Agarwal,
who translated the German text
of "Frau Holle." —J.W.S.

For Jack, Sam, and Catherine,
born on March 28, 2000 —J.W.

First published in the United States, Great Britain, Canada,
Australia, and New Zealand in 2001 by North-South Books,
an imprint of Nord-Süd Verlag AG, Gossau Zürich, Switzerland.
Distributed in the United States by North-South Books Inc., New York.

Library of Congress Cataloging-in-Publication Data is available.
The CIP catalogue record for this book is
available from The British Library.

ISBN 1-55858-926-0 (TRADE)
1 3 5 7 9 TR 10 8 6 4 2
ISBN 1-55858-925-2 (LIBRARY)
1 3 5 7 9 LE 10 8 6 4 2
Printed in Singapore

For more information about our books, and the authors and artists
who create them, visit our web site: www.northsouth.com

RETELLER'S NOTE

Little children are intrigued with the mystery of snow, and I was no exception. I remember my delight when during story hour a children's librarian introduced me to the magic of Mother Holly shaking her quilt to make snow fall. The story remained a favorite, and as an adult I began to see how it reflected human mystery. Why are some people kind and industrious, and others not? I wanted to retell the story myself because I felt that while it is not that well-known today, it has a lot to offer and can speak to children on many different levels.

A search for variant retellings led me to Alison Lurie's *Clever Gretchen and Other Forgotten Folktales* (Crowell, 1980). That led me to other English-language versions: I discovered Lucy Crane's "Mother Hulda" in *Household Stories* (Dover, 1963), based on the 1886 Grimm edition, Wanda Gag's "Mother Holle" in *More Tales from Grimm* (Coward-McCann, 1947), and Mara Pratt's *Selections from Grimm* (Educational Publishing, 1894), written in the more ornate language used then.

These English retellings made me wonder about the original German-language editions. I found two versions of *Kinder- und Hausmärchen* by Jacob and Wilhelm Grimm: the first, based on the third edition of 1837, "critically revised" by Heinz Rolleke and published by Deutscher Klassiker Verlag in 1985; the second, based on the 1819 edition, also edited by Rolleke and published in 1984 by Eugan Diedrichs Verlag. In each of these there are minor language differences but no major plot additions or deletions.

With these in hand, I was ready to begin my own version. All retellers deal with two elements: vocabulary choices and plot. We choose words so the story reads well aloud. I retained the somewhat obscure term "baker's peel" in the scene where Rose takes the bread from the oven, and I added the repeated sounds of the bramble bush. In addition, I liked describing Mother Holly's teeth as both enormous and dreadful, to convey the idea that appearances can be deceiving.

When it came to the plot, I decided to add a father for Rose, to give her a reason for wanting to return home. I included both girls meeting the cow, part of only the Lurie edition based on an 1884 Grimm edition. In all previous editions, pitch or tar fell on Blanche. Because that would be difficult to remove, I changed it to barbs, bristles, and burrs, which are miserable but not impossible to remove. Finally, I added the episode of the two girls returning to Mother Holly, where Rose teaches Blanche the meaning of the word *industrious*. That reinforces my belief, useful to children, that with help we can all change the way we behave.

ONCE, LONG AGO AND FAR AWAY, lived a woman with two daughters. One, named Rose, was pretty and industrious, always busy sewing, washing, and cleaning. The other, named Blanche, was mean and lazy, always busy complaining, whining, and objecting. But strangely enough the woman loved Blanche, her own daughter, better. And she so disliked Rose, her stepdaughter, that she forced her to be the drudge of the house. Rose's father could do nothing about this sorry state of affairs. From the first ray of the sun until the first star of evening he toiled, trying to satisfy all his wife's and stepdaughter's extravagant demands.

Every day Rose had to sit by the well near the high road and spin until her fingers bled. Now it happened one day that a drop of blood fell on the spindle. Rose dipped the spindle into the well to wash it, but it slipped out of her hand and fell in. Then she began to cry, and she ran to her stepmother, who raged and said, "You let the spindle fall in, so you must go and fetch it out."

The poor girl went back to the well, and not knowing how else to solve her problem, jumped down the well after the spindle.

Now this was no ordinary well, so Rose did not drown. Rather she knew nothing until she awoke lying in a meadow, with the sun shining brightly and thousands of beautiful flowers around her.

As she walked along, she came upon a baker's oven, and at once the loaves of bread began to talk. "Oh, take us out, take us out or we shall scorch, for we are baked to a turn already."

So Rose, feeling sorry for the bread, did as she was asked. Using a baker's peel, she removed the loaves, stacking them neatly beside the oven. "Please," she asked, "may I take just one loaf to eat as I walk along? For the sun is high and it is a long time since breakfast."

After walking for a time, she came to a tree, heavily weighted down with a huge crop of apples. "Oh, shake me, shake me," the tree said, "for my branches are near to breaking with ripe fruit."

So Rose, concerned about the tree, shook a branch until the apples fell like rain. When no more were left on the tree, she piled them neatly beside the trunk. Then she asked, "Please, may I take one apple to eat as I go along? For I have come a long way, and don't know when I shall get home again."

After walking for a time, she came to a cow grazing in a field. "Oh, milk me, milk me," the cow said, "for my udder is heavy and full and it makes me uncomfortable." So Rose, compassionate at the cow's plight, milked her. Then Rose asked, "Please, may I have a drink of your milk to quench my thirst, for the day is very hot."

At last she came to a little cottage. The window was open, and leaning on the sill was an old woman. She looked pleasant enough, but she had enormous teeth, which frightened Rose.

"Come here, little girl, so we may talk," said the woman. "Don't be afraid. My name is Mother Holly." After Rose told the woman her name, Mother Holly said, "If you should care to stay with me, and help me with my housework, all would go well with you." She spoke so kindly that Rose asked what her work would be.

"You must keep my cottage clean, and take special care to make my bed nicely every morning. You must shake it up until the feathers fly, so it will snow on earth. If you serve me well, you won't regret it."

So Rose stayed with Mother Holly, despite her dreadful teeth. Rose worked hard, as was her habit, and every morning she shook the mattress so that the feathers flew around like snowflakes.

Mother Holly treated her well. The girl never heard a harsh word, and they had roast meat every night for supper.

Time passed pleasantly enough, but after a long while Rose grew sad. Even though her life at home had been hard, she longed to return. So she said, "You have been very good to me, but I am homesick. I used to grieve about my troubles. But even if they all come again, I still want to go home and see my father."

"Of course, my dear," said Mother Holly. "It is good that you should want to do so. Because you have served me so faithfully, I will help you return home." From a chest she took a golden dress and put it on Rose, and she gave her the spindle she had lost. She took her to a secret door that Rose had never noticed before. As Rose passed through, gold came raining down from above, covering her from top to toe.

"That's your reward for helping me," said Mother Holly.

Mother Holly shut the door and Rose found herself in the world
again, not far from her father's house. Her father hugged her and wept
for joy, for he had thought his beloved daughter dead.

The stepmother was not so happy, but concealed her real feelings,
making a fuss over Rose because of all that gold.

The next morning the stepmother determined that her own, mean, lazy daughter, Blanche, should have the same fortune. "Go to the well to spin," the stepmother ordered. She even pushed the girl's hand into a bramble bush so it would bleed. "Now throw the spindle in, and jump after it, and we shall see what we shall see," her mother said.

Blanche awakened in the same meadow as her sister had. As she walked, she came to the baker's oven full of bread, and at once the loaves began to talk.

"Oh, take us out, take us out or we shall scorch, for we are baked to a turn already."

But Blanche said, "Why should I? I have no desire to get my hands dirty. Besides, at home I feast on fine white rolls and rich cakes. I have no need of common bread."

So saying, she stuck her nose in the air and walked on.

After a time she came to the tree, heavily weighted down with a huge crop of apples.

"Oh, shake me, shake me, for my branches are near to breaking with ripe fruit."

"Why should I?" asked Blanche. "One of your apples might fall on my head. Besides, at home I don't eat common apples. I insist upon sweet oranges and luscious grapes."

So saying, she stuck her nose in the air and walked on.

Finally she came to the cow, who called out, "Oh, milk me, milk me, for my udder is heavy and full and it makes me uncomfortable."

"Why should I?" asked Blanche. "I might spatter milk on my gown. Besides, at home we drink only the rarest of wines. I have no need of common milk."

At last Blanche came to Mother Holly's house. She was not frightened by Mother Holly's looks, having heard all the details from her stepsister, so she walked boldly in.

"Old woman," she demanded, "give me the best you have to eat and drink, for my journey has been long and my patience has grown short. I've come to stay with you."

The first day Blanche tried to do as Mother Holly told her, for she wanted to be covered with gold, too. But she was not used to hard work and didn't know how to do the commonest chores, so everything went wrong. The second day she slept until the afternoon and was idle the rest of the day. When Mother Holly scolded her, she grew sulky, and so on the third day she was both cross and tired, and cleaned the house badly. When she made Mother Holly's bed, she didn't shake the mattress, so no snow fell on the earth to water it. When spring returned on earth, the fields were dry and barren.

Mother Holly soon had enough of lazy Blanche, so she said, "You have stayed here quite as long as I need you." Secretly, Blanche was glad, for she thought that now she, too, would be covered with a shower of gold. Mother Holly handed Blanche the spindle, and led her to the secret door.

But as Blanche passed through, a tumble of prickles and briars and brambles fell on her. "That's your reward for serving me as you've done," said Mother Holly. She shut the door, and Blanche found herself in the world again, near home. She was not shimmering with precious gold, but covered all over with barbs and bristles and burrs.

When her mother saw her, she shrieked and scolded. She thrust the girl into a tub of hot water, and together they scrubbed until they had worn out their scrubbing brushes. But the stubborn thorns stuck to Blanche. She could neither sit nor lie down in comfort, and made everybody miserable with her.

When she went into the village, the people mocked the spiny girl, bringing even greater remorse to her mother, who knew it was her greed that had brought her daughter to this sad state. Things went on this way until Rose took pity on the unhappy pair. "Let us return to Mother Holly. Perhaps she will agree to help us," she said.

Holding hands, Rose and Blanche jumped into the well together, and when they awoke, they were lying in the meadow side by side.

Mother Holly was once again leaning on her windowsill, and she listened as Rose told of her idea. "You may stay," she responded, "providing you follow your plan."

So the next morning Rose showed Blanche how to scrub the kitchen floor, dust the dining-room chairs, and wash the bedroom curtains. It was all new to Blanche, and she grumbled a lot at the beginning. But by the end of the day one of the prickles had fallen out.

On the second day Rose showed Blanche how to tidy up the pantry, fluff up the settle cushions, and shake the feather bed. Blanche complained less, and several of the brambles fell to the floor.

On the third day Blanche learned how to hoe the garden carrots, gather the eggs, and whitewash the pigsty. In the process, a trail of briars fell off behind her.

At last Mother Holly said, "You've stayed here as long as you need to," and led the girls to the secret door. "Let me reward you as you deserve."

Blanche and Rose walked through, and awoke in the field near their father's house, one as golden as the other.

When the two arrived home, their father and mother rejoiced over
their safe return. Seeing her daughter greatly changed, the mother set
her and Rose to tasks together. Though Blanche was sometimes
tempted to complain, her relieved mother would not allow it.
Rose was delighted to be home and to have an amiable
companion to help with the work. Now her father
could return to his fields without worry,
and so the family prospered.